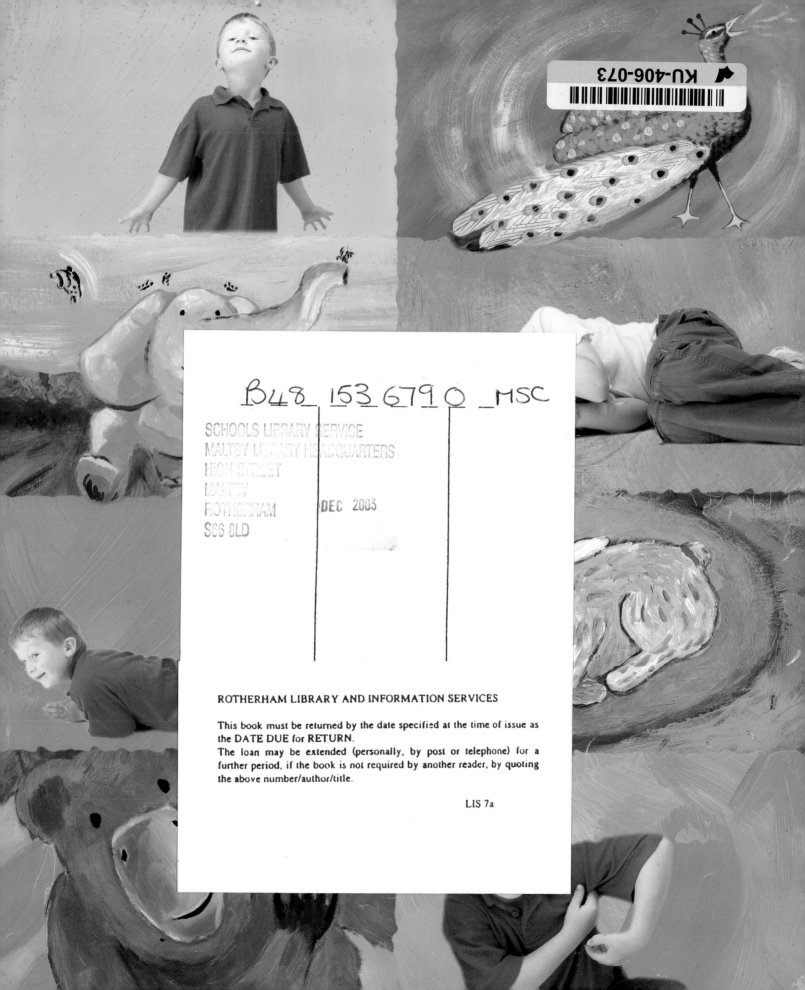

CAN YOU MOVE LIKE AN ELEPHANT?
A DOUBLEDAY BOOK 0385 604084

Published in Great Britain by Doubleday,
an imprint of Random House Children's Books

This edition published 2004

1 3 5 7 9 10 8 6 4 2

Text copyright © Judy Hindley, 2004
Illustrations copyright © Manya Stojic, 2004
Photographs copyright © Roddy Paine 2004

Designed by Ian Butterworth

RANDOM HOUSE CHILDREN'S BOOKS
61–63 Uxbridge Rd, London W5 5SA
A division of The Random House Group Ltd

RANDOM HOUSE AUSTRALIA (PTY) LTD
20 Alfred Street, Milsons Point, Sydney,
New South Wales 2061, Australia

RANDOM HOUSE NEW ZEALAND LTD
18 Poland Road, Glenfield, Auckland 10, New Zealand

RANDOM HOUSE (PTY) LTD
Endulini, 5A Jubilee Road, Parktown 2193, South Africa

THE RANDOM HOUSE GROUP Limited Reg. No. 954009
www.kidsatrandomhouse.co.uk

A CIP catalogue record for this book is available from the British Library.

Printed and bound in China by Midas Printing Ltd

Can You Move Like an Elephant?

Judy Hindley Illustrated by **Manya Stojic**

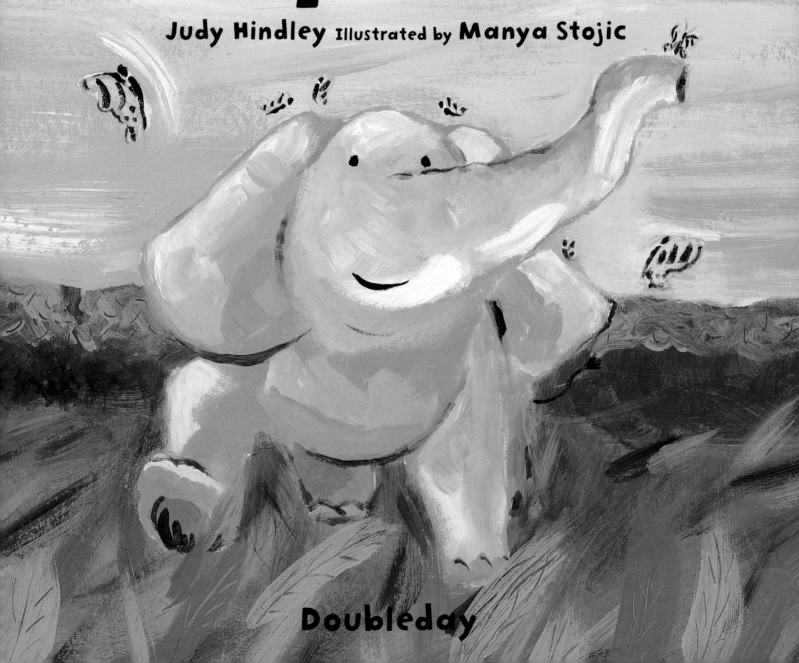

Doubleday

Can you do what an
elephant does?

Deep in the jungle,
the elephants go —
slow, slow, to and fro,
swinging their trunks
from side to side.

Boom!
Boom!

the elephants go.

Can you go
like that?

Can you go like a
slithery snake?
A slithery snake
    curls up so small
and wiggles
and wiggles
and writhes . . .
twisting
her body from
side to side.

Can you leap
out of reach like
a monkey does?
Can you go swinging
from branch to
branch,
and huddle in
snuggly bunches
together
to cuddle and
chatter and
snatch?

Can you do
a monkey
scratch?

Can you hold up
your head like a
peacock does?
Can you walk so proud?
Can you cry so loud?

Awk! Awk!

swishing your
tail from side
to side.

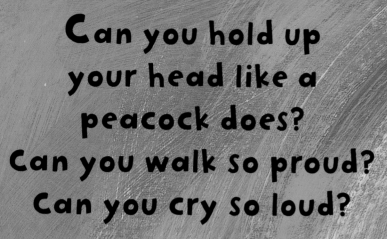

Can you do that?

Can you go as
slow as
a silvery
snail,
reaching
and
searching with
delicate horns,
stretching
his stone-
coloured,
moon-coloured
body,
long
and skinny and slim?

And then can you **QUIVER** as quick as a flame like a butterfly wavering, flower to flower, silently flickering **big**, bright wings?

Can you do that?

Can you go
like a tiger goes,
silently stalking
her prey —
slinking
ever so
slowly and
low to the
ground ...
till she crouches
and
springs
in a glorious bound?

Can you
do that?

And can you go
like a startled
deer,
when she
picks up her head
and
FREEZES
with
fear —
and then goes
springing
away?

Can you
do that?

Can you wheel and whirl like a terrified herd, when the tiger is following faster and faster;

turn on your hooves all together like dancers, and slip like the wind from her pursuit?

Can you shift and turn like that?

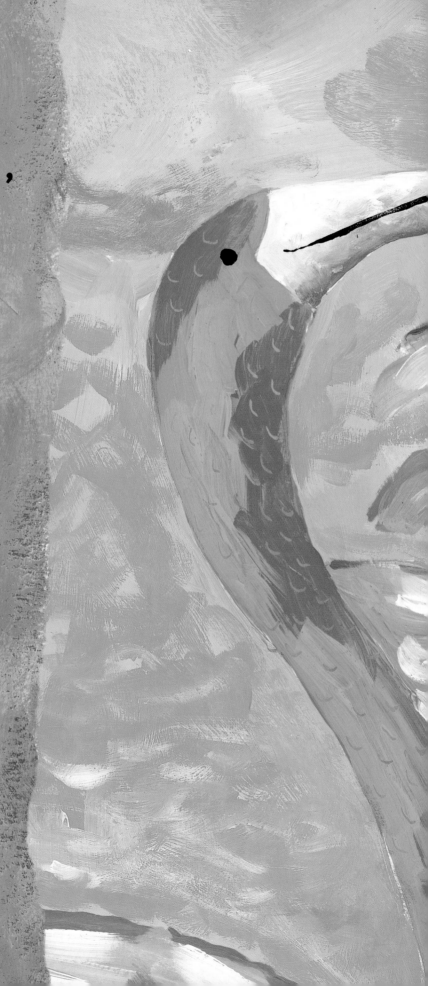

Can you lift
your wings like
huge flamingos,
brushing
their feathers
like fingers
together,
in ripples of
colour that cover
the sun,
circling the sky
until danger is
gone?

Can you ripple
and swing
like that?

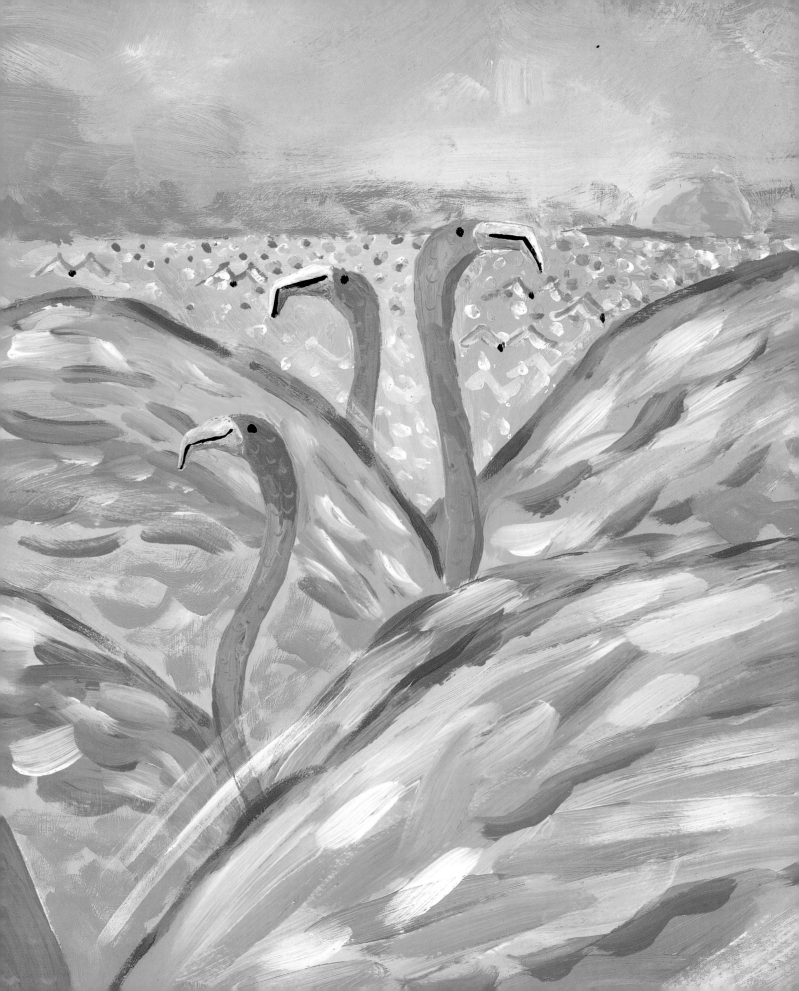

And can you go like
a small, grey rabbit,
who dives in his
burrow and sinks
to his rest,
settling soft as a
small, grey cloud,
with his head
bending gently
to his
chest?

Can you be as
quiet and peaceful
as that?

Can you sleep so
sweet
at the end of the
day?

Can you sleep
like that?